The Discontented Gopher

The Discontented Gopher

by L. Frank Baum

Illustrated by Carolyn Digby Conahan

A Prairie Tale

SOUTH DAKOTA STATE HISTORICAL SOCIETY PRESS

PIERRE

A PRAIRIE TALE FROM THE
SOUTH DAKOTA STATE HISTORICAL SOCIETY PRESS

Editor: Nancy Tystad Koupal
Designer: Mark Conahan
Production Manager: Patti Edman
To Mark, for saying: "You have to draw the gopher fairies!" C.D.C.

The text of "The Discontented Gopher" was originally published
in the *Delineator* in March 1905.

This publication is funded, in part, by
the Great Plains Education Foundation, Aberdeen, S.Dak.

Library of Congress Cataloging-in-Publication Data

Baum, L. Frank (Lyman Frank), 1856-1919.

The discontented gopher / by L. Frank Baum; illustrated by Carolyn Digby Conahan.

p. cm.

"A Prairie Tale from the South Dakota State Historical Society Press."
Summary: Zikky, a young descendant of the Thirteen-lined Gophers of America, finds
more adventure than he bargained for when, bored with guarding the treasure he found as
a gift of the Gopher Fairies, he ignores their warning to avoid "the abodes of men."
Includes bibliographical references, historical notes, and word list.
ISBN 0-9749195-9-4 (alk. paper)
[1. Fairy tales. 2. Gophers – Fiction. 3. Contentment – Fiction.
4. Prairies – Fiction. 5. South Dakota – Fiction.] I. Conahan, Carolyn, ill. II. Title.
PZ8.B327Dis 2006
[E] – dc22   2006007032

Printed in Canada

10 09 08 07 06   1 2 3 4 5

Introduction

"THERE IS NO good reason," wrote L. Frank Baum, why fairy tales should not be set in America. And so he wrote fairy tales about the people and animals who lived on the hills and plains of the United States. He called his stories "wonder-tales." His most famous one was about a girl named Dorothy who traveled with a scarecrow, a tin woodman, and a lion. It is called *The Wizard of Oz*. Dorothy grew up in Kansas. When she looked out of her house, she saw that "not a tree nor a house broke the broad sweep of flat country that reached the edge of the sky in all directions."

How did Baum know what the prairies looked like? He never lived in Kansas. But he did live two states north of Kansas in South Dakota. He ran a store and owned a newspaper in the town of Aberdeen. Some of his family owned a farm a few miles farther north on the prairies of North Dakota. Many people think that Baum was thinking of the two Dakotas when he wrote the first pages of the *Wizard of Oz*. We know that he had South Dakota in mind when he wrote *The Discontented Gopher*. It is set on the prairie and farms outside of Aberdeen.

Farms were new on the prairies of Dakota. Before Baum and others moved there, American Indian tribes such as the Lakotas lived on the American plains. These people were nomads. They moved from place to place and hunted the buffalo and other wild game that lived in the Great Plains. They gathered wild plants to add to their diets. Some tribes planted crops along the rivers, but most did not. Like the plants and the animals, the land was left to grow wild. When Baum and the new settlers entered South Dakota from the east, they plowed the land and planted crops all across the state.

To the wild animals that lived on the plains, these crops were riches to be eaten and saved up for winter. Gophers were especially fond of wheat and corn. They soon grew fat on all the new food. They moved onto the farms and ate the green leaves of the growing corn. They ate the stalks of the plants. They nibbled on the kernels of corn before they were ripe. All in all, they ate as much as a third of the farmers' crops. They were taking food from the farmers and their families. Something had to be done about them! That is the background for the story that Baum tells in *The Discontented Gopher*. It is about a little thirteen-lined ground squirrel, or gopher.

The farmers and the people who lived in towns like Aberdeen made a plan to get rid of the gophers. They would pay people a bounty for each gopher tail brought into town. Many young people trapped gophers to make spending money. They did it during recess at school or during the summer vacation. Baum's own son, Robert, hunted gophers on his cousin's farm in North Dakota during the summers. When Baum wrote this story in 1905, the bounty for gopher tails in Aberdeen was two cents. There were so many gophers that one boy trapped one hundred gophers in one day. He made two dollars. The plan helped to reduce the number of gophers so that people could bring in good crops. But it was hard on the gophers, as this story shows. Baum did not like to see animals suffer. This story also looks at how we make choices and how we learn to live with the bad choices we make.

Baum had a gift for telling stories. He looked at the small things of everyday life and turned them into something special. He took the American prairies and breathed magic into them. In his stories, gophers can talk; scarecrows can walk; and wizards live in Omaha. Baum wrote fourteen stories about Americans who found their way to Oz. He also wrote fairy tales set in the Dakotas and other American places.

The Discontented Gopher

DAWN BEGAN to lighten the sky. Mama Gopher stuck her head out of the burrow and sniffed the clear, sweet air. There was no taint of Man or animal in the breath, so she whisked from the hole and paused a yard or two away, on the summit of a little knoll.

Before her lay a broad sweep of Dakota prairie, whose dull brown color the Spring was tinting with suggestions of emerald. Far away – miles and miles, it seemed in the clear atmosphere – there were glimpses of plowed fields even now ready for the planting. But the day was too new for sight of men.

Mama Gopher whisked her bushy tail, thoughtfully stroked her nose with her front paw, and uttered a little chirruping cry:

"Britz, come here!"

A streak of tawny amber flashed from the burrow, and a young Gopher, half grown, sleek and plump, squatted beside its mother. She gazed upon it, meditated a moment, and called again:

"Kritt! Zikky!"

A slight scuffle reached her ears, as if the children contended which should be first to answer. Then two more young ones joined

the group on the knoll, so swiftly and silently that Mama Gopher had
to look at each one to be sure it was there.

"The time has come," she began, in a brisk, matter-of-fact tone, "for
you three youngsters to start out in life and seek your own fortunes.
I have cared for you faithfully during the Winter, as a mother should,
and you have lain in my burrow and eaten of my store until the
hole has grown crowded, and the food is nearly gone. Moreover, it is
Spring, and time to be moving. We have slept all the Winter through,
and grown lazy and fat. We must be going."

"I am ready," said Britz.

"And I! and I!" cried Kritt and Zikky, eagerly.

"Then listen to me," resumed the mother, more gravely. "You are the direct descendants of the Original Thirteen-Lined Gophers of America—famed for ages in song and story. Because of your high birth I went yesterday to the Gopher Fairies and implored them to grant a gift to each of my three offspring. But the Fairies are busy and have many demands upon them, so numerous are the Gophers now in existence. Yet they granted me a single magic talisman, which is contained in one of the three nuts you see before you."

The children looked, and saw at Mama Gopher's feet three beautiful nuts lying upon the ground.

"You are the eldest, my dear Britz," she continued; "you shall choose first."

Britz selected a nut and cracked it with his teeth. It was empty, save for a few grains of dust.

"The Fairy gift is not for you," said the mother. "So bid us goodbye, my dear, and start out to seek your own fortune."

A moment later Britz shot out of sight, and Mama Gopher, after following him with her eyes, sighed and turned to the next child.

"You are the second, Kritt. Choose one of the nuts."

This the youngster did, but when he cracked his nut it was found to be as empty as the first.

"Goodbye! I'm off," he shouted, laughingly, and whisked away through the tall prairie grass.

This left Zikky, the youngest, facing his mother upon the knoll and looking longingly at the remaining nut.

"Your brothers, by selecting the wrong nuts, have given you the prize," said the old Gopher, with mingled tenderness and regret in her tones. "Crack it, Zikky, and see what is inside."

Zikky cracked the nut, and a tiny golden ball rolled out.

"This ball," said the mother, "will grant you one of two things: Contentment or Riches. Which will you select, Zikky?"

"Riches, to be sure!" cried the young one, promptly; "for there can be no Contentment without Riches."

"The Fairies think differently," said Mama Gopher; "and I myself must doubt the wisdom of your choice. But it is too late to alter your decision now, and you must abide by it!"

"That I will do right gladly," was the answer.

"Then swallow the ball and follow the golden pathway that will lead to Fortune. It is the gift of the generous Gopher Fairies, and I trust you will use your riches with a wisdom and dignity worthy of your noble ancestors. Goodbye, my child!"

With these words Mama Gopher darted into her burrow, and Zikky was left alone.

Immediately he swallowed the golden ball, and no sooner had he done so than he saw an illumined path, like a ray of golden sunshine, running from his feet straight out into the prairie and far away.

ALONG THIS PATHWAY he darted. Fortune, granted him by the good Fairies, lay at the other end. How lucky he had been – and how wise his choice!

Up hill and down dale, through meadow-land and sagebrush the golden path faithfully led him. It was a long journey, and the instincts of his race kept Zikky alert. His eyes were bright and sharp, and saw everything as he ran. His nose was slightly uplifted that he might scent any danger that came anigh. The birds, perhaps, saw a yellow streak glide swiftly through the clumps of dried grass – following a bar of golden light – but no other thing upon the vast prairie knew that Zikky the Gopher was making a dash into the world to seek a home and fortune, or that he was guided by the powerful Fairies of his race.

Finally, as he topped a small ridge, the sun began to show over the horizon, and the golden pathway grew gradually more dim. Presently it led him to the edge of a plowed field, just below the brow of a hill, and there it ended in a round disk of mellow light.

While he paused, wondering what to do next, and where he should find the promised riches, a Voice sounded clearly in his ear:

"Dig here your burrow, and riches shall come to you. But it will be your task to secrete them, as well as to guard them when your treasure house is full and overflowing. Beware of the abodes of men, which lie over the hill. Remain upon this spot; be vigilant and discreet, and your life and fortune will be safe."

The Voice ceased. Zikky had listened carefully, and now believed he knew what was required of him. At once he tore in the sod a round

hole, the size of the golden disk of light, which would be just big enough for his body to pass through. Then he clawed out the earth with both his fore feet, plying them rapidly one after the other until a little heap of loose soil lay on the grass behind him. This he next scattered, until not a trace remained. Gophers are not like prairie dogs; they never leave a rim of earth around their burrows to advertise their whereabouts.

Again our adventurer scratched out a heap of earth, and again he scattered it wide. The sun rose slowly as he worked, but this did not worry him. Men were not likely to be abroad so early.

After an hour's hard labor the hole was deep enough to hide in. There was even room enough for him to turn around in. So Zikky abandoned work for the present and lay within his burrow to rest, while every nerve in his nervous body tingled with the morning's unusual exertions.

Scarcely had he curled himself up and closed his eyes when a peculiar rumbling sound began to be heard, coming, it seemed, from a far distance.

9

"The Fairies are beginning their work," thought Zikky. "I have done my part; it is their turn now." But he opened wide his little round ears and listened intently while the sound grew louder and nearer until it became a perfect roar. The earth trembled; the very air throbbed with noise; then came a sudden stillness. One or two shouts, in Men's voices, followed. He heard the occasional stamp of a horse's hoof. But the fierce rumbling that had made his heart beat so quickly was no longer to be heard.

Zikky was no coward, and he was curious to know what share the Fairies had in this disturbance. Gradually he approached his nose to the opening of his burrow.

The air was tainted with human smells and horsey smells, but also with a smell he loved dearly—the odor of Indian Corn!

Once his nose peeped from the hole his sharp eyes were instantly busy, for they were close beside it. He saw before him—scarcely three feet away—a big wagon loaded full of shelled corn, the most precious thing in all the world to Gophers. A few paces beyond were two Men, carrying baskets of the corn to fill a machine they used for planting it in the earth.

The men had spilled a good deal; the ground before the Gopher hole was thickly strewn with luscious kernels, while more was constantly sifting out between the boards of the wagon-box.

The young Gopher's heart beat high with joyful excitement as he softly withdrew into his burrow. The Riches promised by the Fairies were his! There was fortune enough piled around him to turn any ordinary Gopher's brain!

Yet his joy was tempered with anxiety. "The Riches will come to you, but it shall be your task to secrete them," the unseen Fairy had said. But surely it was too soon to attempt that yet. The monstrous horses hitched to the wagon looked very dreadful to the Gopher, and without doubt the Men would return to fill their baskets anew. So Zikky crowded himself into the furthest confines of his shallow hole and remained quiet throughout the long day.

Toward evening he heard more shouting; the rumbling of the wheels commenced again; but this time the sound grew less and less, until it died away in the distance.

Then Zikky, happy and hungry, crept from his hole, finding the Fairy promise fully realized. The men had not stopped to pick up the scattered corn, and it covered all the ground around the place where the wagon had stood. Zikky nibbled a kernel with much content and satisfaction, and then turned about and resumed his digging.

The moon rose over the ridge and found him still at work, for now he was obliged to scratch the earth from the far end of his long hole. Yet Gophers do not burrow deeply nor far. Six feet of inclined runway, just large enough for him to pass through, led to a circular chamber, roomy but snug. This was Zikky's sleeping place. There was still a storehouse to be built, which he dug beyond his bedroom and

made large and deep, that it might hold the biggest store of treasure that ever yet fell to the lot of a Gopher. Zikky was young and without personal experience, but he inherited from a long line of ancestors an instinct that taught him positively how to make his home and how to provide for his treasure. When the burrow was complete and the loose earth scattered from its mouth Zikky curled himself up and slept until dawn.

Then he began to gather the kernels of corn. There were so many that he filled the great storehouse he had built without securing half the riches. So he built another storehouse on the other side of his living chamber, and began to fill that also.

While at work he heard the rumbling again; but today the wagon stopped at a place a quarter of a mile away, so Zikky had no fear in quietly pursuing his task. When evening came and the men had returned over the hill every grain of the scattered corn had been safely packed away in Master Zikky's storehouses.

Next day the men completed their planting far up on the hill, and they did not appear thereafter. A long silence fell upon field and prairie, and Zikky, nibbling away contentedly from his vast stores, began to realize that he was, in very truth, the richest Gopher in the world.

Ordinarily these little creatures are forced to work hard for a living. Zikky's brothers were even now, doubtless, striving to find a stray grain of corn or a dandelion root to relieve their hunger. But there was no longer need for Zikky to work; his fortune was made already.

So he sat at the mouth of his burrow day after day, dozing in the warmth of the sun and caring little about what might be going on in the outside world. He ate often and plentifully, and became excessively fat.

Then he grew discontented, as people of great wealth and no active interests are apt to do. He began to find existence dull and uninteresting. There seemed to be something lacking, in spite of his riches. He wondered what it could be. He was healthy; he was fat; his home was comfortable; his storehouses would supply food for a lifetime; he had no enemies to bother him.

Yet he was discontented.

MISCHIEF IS SURE to follow this frame of mind; but, being a Gopher, Zikky did not know that. He never even regretted that he had not chosen Contentment instead of Riches. Life had brought him so many pleasures that he believed he could find more.

He came out of his hole one morning, glanced at the low ridge of hills that separated him from "the World," and conceived the idea that led to his undoing.

"I'll travel," he thought, "and see what there is to be seen."

Of course, he remembered what the Fairy Voice had said: "So long as you remain upon this spot your fortune and life will be safe."

But it happens that no discontented person ever heeds good advice. "I saw Men the first day I came to this field," he said to himself, "and I am not at all afraid of them. I saw horses, too, which are much bigger than Men; but they did not harm me. The World lies beyond that ridge, and I am determined to see what it looks like. If I do not like it, I can return. At any rate, the trip will relieve the monotony of my existence."

So next morning he washed his face and brushed his fur and set off at a jog trot for the ridge. The young corn was now growing fast, and reached far above the Gopher's head; so he journeyed between the straight rows until the field was passed and he reached the summit of the ridge. Here he hid himself in a clump of grass while he took his first look at what was to him "the World."

There were roads leading down into the valley beyond, and there were scattered farmhouses, barns and granaries. In the far distance was a larger cluster of houses—a village. Zikky gazed at everything with much interest, and the scene seemed so peaceful that he gained new courage.

"There is nothing to frighten one, after all," thought he; "I'll go down into the Valley, and examine those buildings."

On he trotted, growing more bold and careless the farther he went. Once he looked a bit shyly at a herd of cows grazing in a pasture, but they paid no attention to him. The day was warm and pleasant, and the Gopher forgot the discontent that had haunted him so many days, and became quite cheerful and happy.

Suddenly a strange sound, fraught with terror new and awful, smote his ears. Zikky, roused from his dream of vainglory and self-conceit, stopped short, trembled in every limb, and looked behind.

Bounding toward him was a beast he instinctively recognized as a fierce and furious foe.

Then his own muscles tightened; his body shot forward, and like a streak he darted over the fields. The dog was between the Gopher and the ridge, so Zikky was running through a strange country. He had little time to note where he was going, and having passed a group of farm buildings he came full upon a Man, who was looking to see what game his dog was following. The Gopher acted from instinct and circled swiftly around the Man, who hurriedly pointed a gun at him. There came a flash, a thunderous echo, and as the hunted animal dashed on he felt a stinging sensation in his hip that made him sick and faint.

But he knew he must run, run, run for dear life. Death encompassed him in many forms, turning the Valley of Peace he had so lately traversed into a Valley of Fear. His brain was in a whirl; his heart swelled painfully within him, and the strain upon his muscles grew into a dull ache. There was time for neither hope nor despair. One idea alone possessed him—to run from the danger behind.

Once again he gave a fearful glance over his shoulder. The dog was nearer—coming straight on with lowered head and swift, powerful strides. The sight gave Zikky an access of fear; the fear gave him renewed speed.

Despite the terror and agony of that awful run the Gopher's instinct was awake, leading him to quickly spy a burrow that appeared in his path—a big, round hole slanting far into the earth. Instantly he popped within it, to fall upon the damp floor panting, trembling and exhausted.

The hound barked sharply without; there was a shrill whistle, and then silence.

Lying prone in the darkness and recovering by convulsive gasps his breath, the foolish Gopher began to long for the peaceful home and the riches he had deserted. Already he had seen enough of the world of men to decide it was no place for one of his race. He would return to his burrow as soon as he could find strength and opportunity.

As the beating of his heart grew less he began to wonder what sort of burrow had given him refuge. It belonged to no Gopher; that was certain. It was too big and deep. He crawled along the underground tunnel slowly and carefully, for it was strangely built, twisting this way and that in a remarkable manner.

Finally he saw daylight ahead, and knew that for some reason the burrow had two outlets. But he did not approach this second opening. He had not fully recovered from his fright, and the stinging in his hip was becoming more and more painful. So he lay quietly and dozed until there came a sudden rush behind him—so sudden that before he could move to escape his neck was seized between two rows of sharp teeth and he was dragged to the opening and thrust upon the open prairie.

Had the dog been present the Gopher's story would have ended then; but the hound's master had called him away, thinking a Gopher too insignificant to bother with.

Zikky was the descendant of the noble family of Thirteen-Lined Gophers of America, who are tough and hard to kill. Although nearly choked by the indignant Jack-Rabbit whose burrow he had invaded, he managed by persistent struggles to regain his breath. Then he realized the danger of his exposed position. Strengthened by fear, he gained his feet and looked about him.

The ridge he had crossed so confidently a short time before was visible in the distance; but between that haven of safety and the wounded Gopher stood the group of farm buildings. Zikky noted this, and stepped painfully forward, determined to give the buildings plenty of room and so escape the chance of meeting more men or dogs. He was not in condition to travel swiftly. His neck smarted; his hip burned like fire, and the muscles of his legs ached from his hard run. Yet his life depended upon gaining the ridge unobserved.

After a while he came to the edge of a dry ditch, and into this

he dropped, crawling along the bottom until he began to fear it was carrying him in the wrong direction, and out of his way. When he had managed to scramble out, he found that he had passed the dreaded farm buildings; but the ridge was still a long distance off. He began walking toward it, stopping often to breathe and keeping well under cover of the grass clumps.

Hope was beginning to animate the poor animal when it was turned to renewed terror by the sound of shouting. He paused in his painful, shuffling gait, and saw two farm boys running toward him. He tried to make another dash for liberty, but he was weak and ill. Before he had gone more than a few yards a thick stick, hurled by one of the boys, struck his head. He fell over upon his side and lay still.

"Good shot!" cried the other boy, as he ran to the Gopher and picked him up by his bushy tail. "You hit him fair and square."

"He was nearly dead, anyhow," replied the one who had thrown the stick. "See, something has bitten him; and he's been shot, too. I'll just cut off his tail and put it with the others I have, in the barn. They pay a bounty of two cents apiece for Gopher tails, in Aberdeen. This makes nine of 'em I've killed in a week."

(Two cents apiece for Gopher tails! That means a Gopher's life. Is it really worth while, I wonder, to write so much about one of God's creatures whose life is worth only two cents?)

The proud slayer of nine Gophers in one week took a clasp-knife from his pocket and with a quick stroke severed the tail from Zikky's body. Then he threw the Gopher into the grass and walked away with his comrade.

4.

WHEN THE MOON came up the tailless body jerked once or twice, in a spasmodic fashion, and Zikky's eyes slowly unclosed. It is hard to kill one of his race. The Thirteen-Lined Gophers of America seem to possess as many lives as a cat is said to have. He was full of darting pains, and his head was dazed. But he remembered, in a dim way, that he must reach the ridge. Slowly he began to crawl toward it.

"What good are my riches now?" he moaned, time and again. "I should have chosen the Gift of Contentment; it would have saved me this!"

The moonlight enabled him to see. The dew fell heavily and refreshed his strength. His courage was the courage of a line of ancestors who had ever clung to life with marvelous tenacity. But it was a journey Zikky never forgot, and the agony he suffered during that moonlit night effaced from his mind even the horrors that had gone before.

In some way—how, he never knew—he gained the ridge, dragged himself through the cornfield and came at early dawn to his burrow. He crawled in until he reached the roomy chamber flanked by his overflowing storehouses of grain, and there he curled his maimed body and sank, sobbing and broken-hearted, into a sleep of utter exhaustion.

The Fairy gift Zikky had formerly scorned had come to him at last; but at what terrible cost!

"Contentment is best! Contentment is best!" he often murmured, in the days that followed. "Some day I shall seek out my mother and tell her I was wrong, and that riches do not bring Contentment."

But he never did. For he grew ashamed of his tailless stump, and when other Gophers strayed into his neighborhood, as sometimes happened thereafter, Zikky would only stick his head and shoulders from his hole, conversing with them, when conversation could not be avoided, while in that position.

"He is proud of his wealth, and stuck-up, and conceited!" the Gophers declared, as they went away.

But Zikky was only ashamed.

Bibliography

Baum, L. Frank. *American Fairy Tales*. Indianapolis: Bobbs–Merrill, 1908.

Baum. *Animal Fairy Tales*. Chicago: International Wizard of Oz Club, 1969.

Baum. *Twinkle and Chubbins: Their Astonishing Adventures in Nature-Fairyland*. Intro. Michael Patrick Hearn. N.p.: International Wizard of Oz Club, 1987.

Brown County History. Aberdeen, S.Dak.: Brown County Museum & Historical Society, 1980.

Carpenter, Angelica Shirley, and Jean Shirley. *L. Frank Baum: Royal Historian of Oz*. Minneapolis: Lerner Publications Co., 1992.

Early History of Brown County, South Dakota: A Literature of the People by Territorial Pioneers and Descendants. Aberdeen, S.Dak.: Brown County Territorial Pioneer Committee, 1965.

Hearn, Michael Patrick, ed. Introduction to *The Annotated Wizard of Oz*. Centennial Ed. New York: W. W. Norton & Co., 2000.

Koupal, Nancy Tystad, ed. *Baum's Road to Oz: The Dakota Years*. Pierre: South Dakota State Historical Society, 2000.

Word list

abide – live
abodes – houses; living spaces
ancestors – family members from the past
anigh – near
animate – bring to life
bounty – reward
conceited – overly pleased with oneself
convulsive – jerking
contentment – happiness; peace of mind
descendants – offspring
discreet – careful
effaced – erased; wiped out
exertions – efforts
Indian corn – maize; yellow corn
illumined – lighted up
knoll – a small hill
monotony – dull routine; boredom
persistent – staying at something; lasting
secrete – hide
smote – hit
spasmodic – moving in short, quick jerks
summit – the highest point; top
taint – a trace of something bad
talisman – a charm
tenacity – stubbornness; ability to hold fast
traversed – traveled across
vainglory – too much pride